Puffin Books

Professor Branestaw
Mouse War

When Professor Branestawm declared war on the mice in his house, Mrs Flittersnoop knew that trouble was on the way. The Professor devised ingenious traps and potions to rid his house of the menace – some of which had some very peculiar results – but nothing worked. The mice wouldn't budge and the problem rapidly went from bad to worse. Then the Professor invented the most wonderful mouse-scarer of all time. But would it work? Anyone who's ever heard of Professor Branestawm's incredible inventions would have their doubts!

Several people had doubts too about the Professor's solution to Great Pagwell's housing problem but, for once, he appeared to have produced a truly amazing invention – instant houses! However, not all was quite as it seemed, and soon the bricks and cement began to fly!

Professor Branestawm's Mouse War and *Professor Branestawm's Building Bust-up* were specially written for young readers and are published together for the first time in this book.

NORMAN HUNTER

Professor Branestawm's Mouse War

Illustrated by Gerald Rose

PUFFIN BOOKS

PUFFIN BOOKS

Published by the Penguin Group
27 Wrights Lane, London w8 5tz, England
Viking Penguin Inc., 40 West 23rd Street, New York, New York 10010, USA
Penguin Books Australia Ltd, Ringwood, Victoria, Australia
Penguin Books Canada Ltd, 2801 John Street, Markham, Ontario, Canada l3r 1b4
Penguin Books (NZ) Ltd, 182–190 Wairau Road, Auckland 10, New Zealand

Penguin Books Ltd, Registered Offices: Harmondsworth, Middlesex, England

Professor Branestawm's Mouse War first published by The Bodley Head Ltd 1982
Professor Branestawm's Building Bust-up first published by The Bodley Head Ltd 1982
Published in one volume in Puffin Books 1984
Reprinted 1988

Made and printed in Great Britain by
Richard Clay Ltd, Bungay, Suffolk
Filmset in Monophoto Plantin

Contents

Professor Branestawm's
Mouse War

Mrs Flittersnoop, Professor Branestawm's housekeeper, was on the telephone. At least she was not actually on the telephone, but was standing on the table beside it – and she was talking to a mouse. The mouse was not on the telephone either. He was sitting on the floor looking up at Mrs Flittersnoop, who was in a dither or two.

'Professor,' she called, 'come quickly! There's a mouse in the house!'

Professor Branestawm came rushing out of his inventory, his hands full of five pairs of spectacles and three screwdrivers, and his mouth full of nails. He was in the middle of a rather drastic invention.

But the mouse, who didn't mind talking to ladies standing on telephone tables, didn't care much for talking to professors with their hands full of screwdrivers. So he nipped down his private mousehole a bit smartish.

'You really must do something about the mice,' said Mrs Flittersnoop, climbing off the table. 'That's the third this week.'

'Well, um, ah, it may not be the third *mouse*,' said the Professor. 'It may just be the same mouse that you have seen three times. But I shall invent a special mouse-trap, all the same.'

He went back to his inventory and, after a lot of banging and scraping and other inventing noises, the first Branestawm Mousetrap was ready. But it was too big to get out of the inventory, so the Professor had another go.

This time he invented not one but several mousetraps.

'By having various mousetraps,' he explained, 'we can catch several mice at a time and so be rid of them quicker.'

'Yes, indeed, I'm sure, sir,' said Mrs Flittersnoop.

The Professor carefully set the mousetraps, forgot where he had put them, and caught his foot in one the next morning.

'I must make a plan showing where all the traps are,' he said, and went off to do that.

Next day his next-door neighbour, Commander Hardaport (Retired), came to see him and got caught in the dining-room mousetrap.

The Professor got him out of it just in time for the Commander to get caught in another one on the landing.

'Place is like a minefield,' growled the Commander. 'Ought to chart it, y'know.'

So the Professor showed him the map sort of chart he had made so that in future the Commander would know where the traps were. Unless, of course, the Professor moved them and forgot to tell the Commander where they were, which was what he probably would do.

A few days later Mrs Flittersnoop was in another dither. A mouse had been caught in one of the Professor's special traps and she couldn't bear to kill it.

So she took it out into Pagwell Park and
let it go. But it followed her home.

The Professor was in a lot of dithers too that day. Every single one of his traps had caught a mouse and some had caught several. But the mice liked the traps so much they were setting up homes in them.

They were sitting in little mice chairs in them, reading mice books and watching mice serials on miniature television sets.

'Oh my goodness!' cried Mrs Flitter-snoop. 'Instead of getting rid of our mice, these traps have attracted other people's!'

'I shall invent an anti-mouse powder,' said the Professor. 'They won't like the smell of it and they'll go away.'

But the mice loved the anti-mouse powder. They not only thought it smelt nice, they thought it tasted nice too.

They had it for breakfast, dinner and supper. They even invented special recipes for using it.

But oh dear! Although the anti-mouse powder didn't get rid of the mice, it turned them different colours.

There were now red-and-green-striped mice, blue-spotted ones and ones with rainbow-coloured patches.

'We must get cats!' cried the Professor rushing to the telephone and falling over Mrs Flittersnoop's cat, who was cautiously studying a saucer of milk from all directions before drinking it.

The cats came in dozens and hundreds in reply to the Professor's appeal.

Cat lovers and cat homes sent them, and some boat people even sent a catamaran, which was no use at all, though they had meant to be helpful.

'Now we shall soon be rid of the mice,' said the Professor.

'Yes, indeed, I do hope so, sir,' said Mrs Flittersnoop.

But none of the cats had ever seen coloured, striped and spotted mice before. They rather liked them. Some of the motherly cats even let the mouse mothers out of the traps to go for walks, while they mouse-sat for them.

So the Professor invented a mechanical cat and an armour-plated mouse-catcher. But those didn't seem to frighten the mice either.

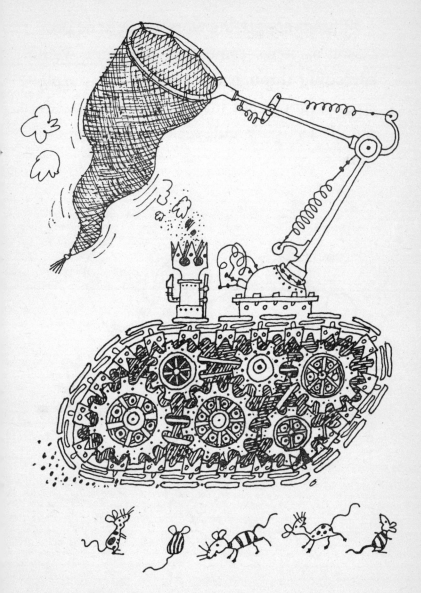

'Things are getting worse!' cried the Professor as news came that the mice were spreading through the Pagwells. A purple striped mouse got into Doctor Mumpzanmeazle's surgery and stuck its tongue out at him.

Two spotted mice went shopping at
Great Pagwell Supermarket and scared the
customers.

'If only I could blow up the mice without blowing up Pagwell,' groaned the Professor. Then he clapped his hand to his head, missed and knocked off three pairs of spectacles.

'That's it!' he cried. 'I shall blow up an enormous balloon in the shape of a terrifying cat. It will scare the mice, um, ah, away.'

He persuaded the Pagwell Furnishing
Company to give him the big plastic bags
that they used to cover furniture. With help
from friends and neighbours, he stuck these
together so they formed one enormous bag

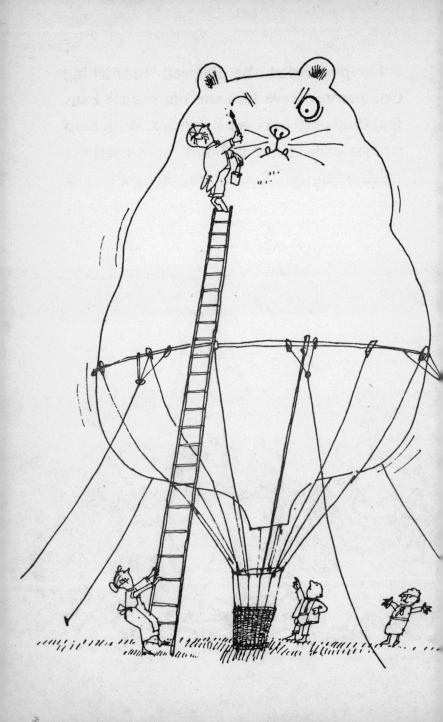

which he blew up like a giant balloon. He
tied a spare basket that he found at the Pagwell Laundry beneath it, and then painted
a huge and frightening face of a cat on the
balloon.

'Now!' cried the Professor, when the huge cat balloon was finished at last and ready to be launched. 'Mice beware!' He jumped into the basket, the guy ropes were untied, and the balloon sailed upwards with all the people of Pagwell cheering below.

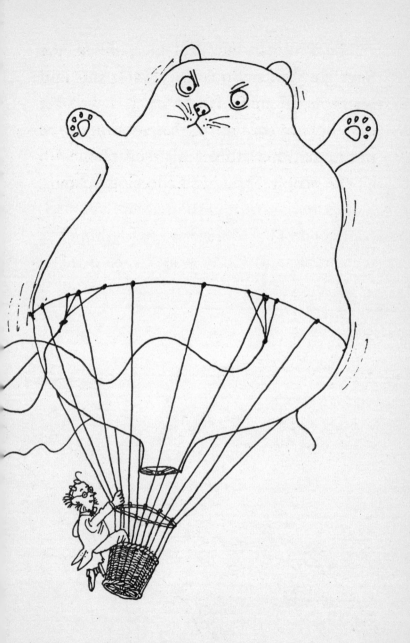

The Professor steered the balloon over Pagwell Market Square. It was rush-hour for shopping mice. He swooped down over the hordes of mice. '*Meeeeeeeow*,' he shouted at them through a megaphone.

The striped, spotted and coloured mice looked up in striped, spotted and coloured confusion. They'd never seen anything like that before and didn't want to see it then.

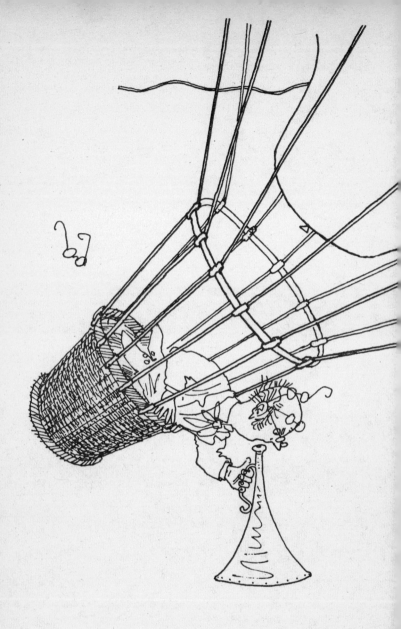

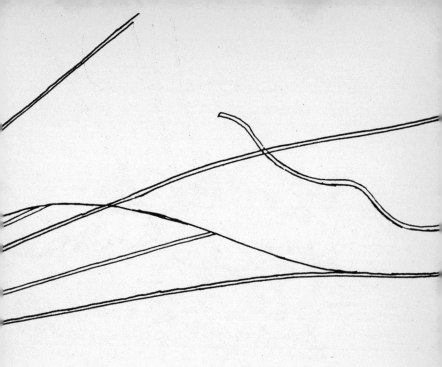

Scamper scamper, rapetty rapetty, scratch, squeak, ow ow! They ran like the seven winds of goodness knows where. And after them went Professor Branestawm in his horrifying cat balloon.

Meeeeeow, grrrrr, hissss. Scampetty, scratch, squeak. The terrified striped, spotted and coloured mice rushed out of Pagwell. They poured through lanes, over meadows and *splosh!* into the River Pag, which swept them away and they were never seen again.

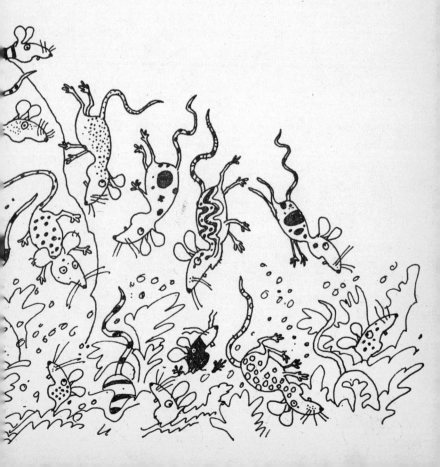

Then the Professor brought his huge cat balloon back down to the ground and gave everyone rides in it to make up for the mice.

'I must, um, ah, say it's very mice not having any nice,' he said, getting his words mixed up.

'Yes, indeed, I'm sure, sir,' said Mrs Flittersnoop, who always knew what the Professor meant.

Professor Branestawm's
Building Bust-up

Great Pagwell was terribly short of houses.
People were having to live with their aunties
because they couldn't find houses of their
own. Families were living in garden sheds,
never mind if the spades and rakes didn't
like it.

Others were living in dog kennels ...

and some in chicken coops. It was awful.

'Something must, um, ah, be done about this shortage of houses,' said Professor Branestawm one afternoooon, clashing his five pairs of spectacles to show he meant it.

'Yes, indeed, I'm sure, sir,' said Mrs Flittersnoop, his housekeeper, as she cleared away the tea things.

'I shall invent a machine that builds houses,' said the Professor, thumping the table and squashing a cream sponge on the tablecloth. Then he went to his inventory to invent a house-building machine and Mrs Flittersnoop went into the kitchen to wash the cream sponge off the tablecloth.

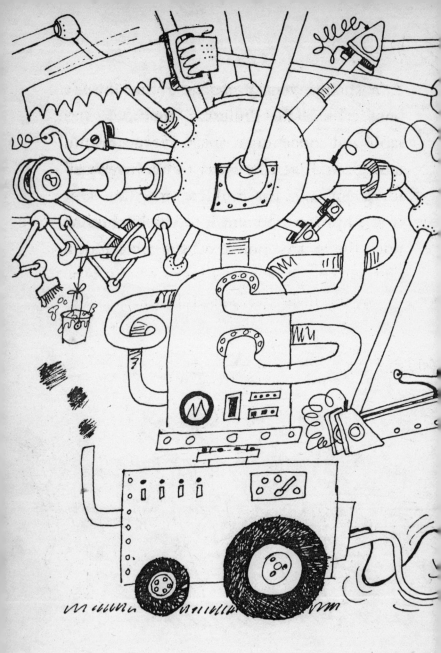

A few days later Professor Branestawm's wonderful house-building machine was ready. It stood on a spare piece of land, surrounded by spare trees and crowds of excited people. Some of the crowd thought it was a space craft and it did look a bit like one. Some thought it was a mechanical octopus and some didn't know what it was.

But the Professor soon told them.

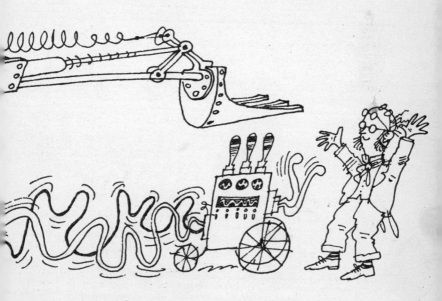

'This, um, ah, machine can build any type of house,' he said to the Mayor of Pagwell, who was there to look important. 'You turn this dial to select the kind of house you want – detached, semi-detached and so on. Then,' he pointed with his spectacles to a bunch of buttons, 'you press these according to how many bedrooms, sitting-rooms, bathrooms and so on you want, and then you pull this lever.'

'Marvellous!' said the Mayor, not believing a word of it.

'I shall now build a detached, three-bedroomed house with two sitting-rooms, kitchen and bathroom,' said the Professor. He turned the dial, pressed buttons and pulled the lever.

Vroom! Puff puff puff, boing! Rattle, bongetty, boom, clank, crash. The machine sprang to life. Wheels whizzed round. Things went up and down and in and out. Clouds of coloured smoke rose up. Piles of bricks and other building stuff were flung in all directions.

'Coo!' said the crowd, dodging in case any bricks came their way.

The house-building noises raged.

Then the dust cleared away and there stood a lovely little house with a red front door, brass knocker and lace curtains.

The Professor looked at the Mayor through three pairs of glasses. The Mayor raised his hat.

'Hurray!' yelled the crowd. They surged
forward. Twenty-seven families tried to get
into the house and got jammed in the front
door. Five other families tried to get in
through the windows, but the windows
wouldn't open.

'Stop, er, um, ah, stop!' cried the Professor. 'Only one family can have this house. You must wait until my machine has built some more.'

But the crowd weren't going to wait. They were tired of living with their aunties, and so were some of the aunties. They were tired of living in garden sheds, dog kennels and chicken coops.

Then they swept the Professor out of the way and grabbed the machine. They twiddled the dial, pressed buttons and pulled the lever ten times a second.

'We want two bed, two sit,' shouted some of the crowd. 'Give us four bed, two sit, one bath,' yelled others. Demands for different houses were hurled into the air as people pressed round the Professor's machine.

Oh dear! Professor Branestawm's inventions were not used to being grabbed by crowds. If it was houses the people wanted, then houses it would give them.

Bang slosh, rattle bang boing, zippetty, slosh. Clouds of dust went up. Bricks flew about. The Mayor had his pockets filled with cement as the machine set to work.

'Stop it!' shouted the Professor, trying to pull a lever and failing.

Bong, bangetty, slap. The machine went whizzing on. Rows and rows of astonishing houses sprang up.

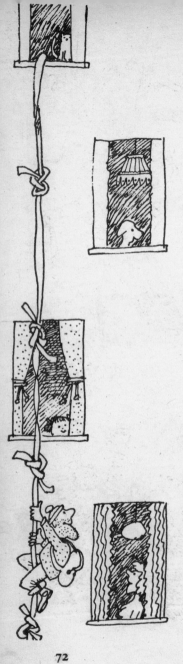

There was one
with seven storeys
and no staircase.

Two had bathrooms on the roof.

Another was shaped like a cheese and would have been lovely for mice.

One landed up a tree . . .

Another house was all doors.

And one shaped
like a wedding
cake was very
sweet.

Another house had the garden inside and the furniture outside, which would be all right in fine weather.

And one house even had a see-through swimming-pool.

The crowd rushed at the houses. They
ran up stairs and fell into bathrooms. But
then the houses started throwing the people
out. *Bong, sloshetty, bong, slap.* People
instead of bricks flew about.

Bong, woosh, splosh, help!

Professor Branestawm made a determined dash at the machine. It dodged him and ran round pulling the houses down. Bricks, cement and tiles rained down.

83

Bang, rattle, crash, boom.

The machine had demolished all the houses! Nothing was left but piles of bricks and wood. Then the astonishing house-building machine sat down and fell apart.

'Well,' said the Professor, scratching his head with two pairs of spectacles. 'The builders can use all these bricks and things to build proper houses and I shall turn my house-building machine into a nice quiet thing for weeding the garden.'

And he went home to think about this over a nice quiet cup of tea.

THE GHOST AT NO. 13
Gyles Brandreth

Hamlet Brown's sister, Susan, is just too perfect. Everything she does is praised and Hamlet is in despair – until a ghost comes to stay for a holiday and helps him to find an exciting idea for his school project!

RADIO DETECTIVE
John Escott

A piece of amazing deduction by the Roundbay Radio Detective when Donald, the radio's young presenter, solves a mystery but finds out more than anyone expects.

RAGDOLLY ANNA'S CIRCUS
Jean Kenward

Made only from a morsel of this and a tatter of that, Ragdolly Anna is a very special doll and the six stories in this book are all about her adventures.

SEE YOU AT THE MATCH
Margaret Joy

Six delightful stories about football. Whether spectator, player, winner or loser these short, easy stories for young readers are a must for all football fans.

Some other Young Puffins

THE DEAD LETTER BOX
Jan Mark

Louie got the idea from an old film which showed how spies left their letters in a secret place – a dead letter box. It was just the kind of thing that she and Glenda needed to help keep them in touch. And she knew the perfect place for it!

THE HA HA BONK BOOK
Janet and Allan Ahlberg

A Young Puffin joke book which is full of good jokes to tell your dad, your mum, your baby brother, your teacher and anybody else you can think of.

THE THREE AND MANY WISHES OF JASON REID
Hazel Hutchins

Jason is eleven and a very good thinker so when he is granted three wishes he is very wary indeed. After all, he knows the tangles that happen in fairy stories!

THE AIR-RAID SHELTER
Jeremy Strong

Adam and his sister Rachel find a perfect place for their secret camp in the grounds of a deserted house, until they are discovered by their sworn enemies and things go from bad to worse.

THE PERFECT HAMBURGER
Alexander McCall Smith

If only Joe could remember *exactly* what he had thrown so haphazardly into the mixing-bowl, he knew that his perfect hamburger could revive his friend Mr Borthwick's ailing business and drive every other fastfood store off the high street. A grand opening announcing the perfect hamburger is arranged – but will Joe and Mr Borthwick find the vital ingredient in time?

THE WORST WITCH
Jill Murphy

Mildred Hubble was a trainee witch and making an awful mess of it. But she managed to get by at Miss Cackle's Academy until she turned Ethel, the teacher's pet, whose spells were always perfect, into her deadly enemy . . .